WALKER ON WATER

Unnamed Press
Los Angeles
www.unnamedpress.com

The stories "Lena of the Drifting Isle", "Walker on Water", "Patterns", "The Dried Apricots of My Six former Husbands" and "Cushions", each originally appeared in English translation in *The Bitter Oleander*.

International Standard Book Number: 978-1-939419-07-1

WALKER ON WATER

Kristiina Ehin

Translated by Ilmar Lehtpere

Unnamed Press
Los Angeles, CA

Acknowledgments

These translations are published with the support of a Traducta grant from the Cultural Endowment of Estonia.

Some of these translations first appeared in *Best European Fiction 2013* (Dalkey Archive Press), *The Bitter Oleander, Molossus, ELM, A Priceless Nest* (Oleander Press) by Kristiina Ehin and *In a Single Breath* (Cross Cultural Communications) by Kristiina Ehin

Contents

Walker on Water

1

The man who later became my husband had many female admirers. They all desired him just as much as I did. There's nothing more exciting than desiring a man who doesn't even notice you.

Jaan is a highly educated man. He works as the director of the Climate Change Monitoring Department at the Academy of Sciences. All of his female admirers have tried to make an impression on him on an intellectual plane, as Jaan's brains are so exceptional.

But I won his heart in a very simple and altogether primitive way. One night I ran to his door stark naked. I said someone had made off with my clothes while I'd gone swimming in the night. Everything went as it went.

So now I'd got in through his door. But my competition still hung about in reading rooms, at round tables and all sorts of seminars.

I glowed with happiness. We went to live at Jaan's ancestral farm. This was Mardi-Jaani farm located at a rather narrow cove between two headlands on the Baltic Sea.

But Jaan's female admirers didn't go anywhere. Even so my belief in Jaan and our love was exceptionally tenacious.

At Mardi-Jaani coastal farm I began again to indulge in my favourite pursuit – walking on water. This demanded the same blind faith and supple strength as loving Jaan did. When Jaan went to work early mornings, I started stepping along the still surface of the sea on the shallow water. I was already managing this quite well. But further from shore I was gripped by fear. And then I sank to the bottom like a stone. I understood that the whole art lay in your ability to completely switch off your brain. You can work wonders with the lightness that then comes. I splashed my way to shore and started again with downy-light liftings of my feet. Without thinking about anything I touched the silver reflection of morning light with the ball of my foot. I was calm, light, sure and focused. I reached the middle of the cove. The tips of the headlands stretched out on either side. I'd reached further than ever before.

That's enough for today. I turn around slowly and walk back to shore.

My marriage is like walking on water too. It's easy if my feet can reach the bottom. It's a game with little danger when everything is just starting out and the little waves lick your shoreline with pleasure.

2

Lately I've discovered that my husband's head opens at the back. I hadn't noticed that before. There's a hatch there. When Jaan comes home after a tiring day at work, he opens the hatch and takes his brains out. They steam on the table, but Jaan stretches his legs out on the sofa and looks at me with his happy, drowsy eyes.

3

I wanted an intelligent and educated man, but what I got was a brainless oaf.

One day a jealous urge awoke in me. I thought that if I can't share in Jaan's brains then they might as well not exist. I suddenly grabbed his brains into my arms and took off running towards the shore in spite of the darkness and the biting wind.

I stepped onto the high crests of the waves. I put all my willpower to work to silence the thumping of my heart, stop my thought processes and keep my balance on the stormy sea. Further out into the deep, still further! Don't lose faith or look at your feet! Over the depths between the two headlands I let go of Jaan's brains. But they had no intention of sinking to the bottom. They bobbed and danced on the crests of the waves just like me.

Jaan stood watching me silently from the shore. I suddenly began to feel sorry for him and myself. That feeling made me weak and heavy. I became frightened. I tried to understand where that fear was coming from. I sank in up to my knees. In a panic I strove to stop my thought processes. I was already splashing about up to my hips, then up to my neck in ice-cold water. I would never be able to swim to shore from here.

I stretched my hands out towards the sky and gasped for air. All at once there was something soft and warm in my hand. I pressed it tightly to my breast. It was Jaan's brains. Suddenly they were keeping me on the surface like a life jacket. I clung to them until the waves had cast us onto the shore.

I felt utterly done for and stiff with cold. Jaan tore his brain from between my hands bent with cramp and set it in its place.

"You're cold, my dear," he said, and put his warm coat around me.

After that he picked me up in his arms and carried me home.

4

I've been trying to keep my love for Jaan afloat. At work he is intelligent and closely surrounded by female admirers. At home in Mardi-Jaani he is totally brain-free. Here I'm the only one he has.

But my ability to walk on the surface of the water is beginning to diminish bit by bit. After just barely managing to stay alive thanks to Jaan's brains while I was trying to drown them, I don't dare go onto the water anymore as easily as before. My belief in myself took quite a beating and I don't stay on the surface so well anymore.

It's the darkest time of the year and everything somehow seems so hopeless. The sea has frozen over and a walker on water has no business there. But as soon as the ice goes, I'm going to try again. In developing my gift I develop my love. Neither can exist without the other.

Patterns

The three men I've bitten arms off of are doing well. I felt guilty for many years. I was afraid I had completely ruined their lives. Of course it must have been difficult for them. But a physical disability doesn't have to make anyone unhappy. If a person has a great will to live, he'll recover from the very greatest traumas.

At times I was quite wild when I was young. I generally managed to keep myself under control in the daytime, but at night I could be a real ferocious beast. My first husband was a very gentle, sensitive man. In the mornings he made thin pancakes fried golden brown in butter and poured coffee mixed with frothed milk into my blue earthenware mug. One morning he just couldn't wait for me to get up. The pancakes were ready and the coffee getting cold. He sat down softly on the edge of my bed and slid his left hand caressingly over my long, soft hair, shoulders and back. I woke with a start. A wild rage came over me. I pounced on to his upper arm and before I understood what I was doing, I had bitten his whole arm off.

When we filed the divorce papers, I cried bitterly. "You could at least have snarled..." he said as he was leaving. "That you suddenly, just like that..."

Jaan is now married to a frail actress. She certainly won't ever bite him. Jaan works at the automobile museum. At open-air events he earns good money with his artificial arm. He sits next to the driver in open

Benzes and De Dion Boutons and points the way, controlling his arm by means of a control panel. In the evening a little light flashes in his arm as well.

Tourists photograph him like mad and Jaan is a made man all over town.

I had therapy for two years and then had the courage to get married again. My second husband's name was also Jaan. We joked that he must be a hard man indeed to take me to be his wife. And himself a discus thrower and the great Olympic hope of the entire nation. It happened already on our wedding night.

As I was expecting a child, I suddenly felt a great tiredness in the midst of all the wedding hubbub. Suddenly I just couldn't dance anymore or sit at the table either. I staggered through the rooms of the hunting lodge we had hired for our wedding reception and climbed the stairs. Jaan was still busy with our guests and an hour later he followed me up to our bedroom. He pushed aside the heavy, white brocade curtains of the canopy bed, kissed me passionately on my half-open lips, opened the hooks on the front of my wedding dress, lay down beside me on the bed and put his right arm under my neck. I felt his gigantic, rapidly twitching muscle. Rage struck me like a thunderbolt. Just as lightning rends a tree with one blow, I had, in a fraction of a second, shattered our people's Olympic hopes. Blood spurted onto the white brocade curtains. Everything all around was suddenly red-white, the approaching ambulance siren rose and fell, the ambulance crew in red overalls stormed in and tried to stop the spurting flow of blood from Jaan's upper arm, lunatic-asylum nurses in white coats wrenched my arms behind my back and led me, with the hooks of my wedding dress open, to the madhouse. Seven months later I gave birth to a dear little girl and got out of the locked ward. For years I lived in the countryside at my grandmother's and helped the old girl with the farmwork. I still took very strong medication. My daughter Maarja was four when we moved back to town. The newspapers didn't write about us anymore.

Jaan married his former beloved just after the accident. Soon after that triplet sons were born to them. Jaan worked at the chocolate factory as a mascot. This job made his family downright wealthy. You see, Jaan had a chocolate arm and was the factory's most expensive attraction. Every evening, when the tour group children had eaten Jaan's arm, a new one was moulded for him. Jaan's sons worshipped their father.

Some years later I met my third husband. For months I tried to convince him that he should find himself a less dangerous woman. But he tried to make me believe that I was completely well. Against my will my daughter Maarja had been waking me in the morning for years and I hadn't attacked her a single time.

We got married in 1998 on St John's day in a close family circle. Maarja was our bridesmaid. My husband – his name was Jaan, too – carried me in his arms to a tiny altar bordered with blossoming lilacs and bird cherry trees at the edge of the forest. Framed by tall fir trees we were joined together under the slanting rays of the evening sun. We pressed wedding rings of genuine raw gold onto each other's finger. They glittered like mad with a wild, dazzling sparkle. Jaan had made the rings himself, he was, after all, a world-famous goldsmith. You would have to look far and wide for a stronger, broader-shouldered man.

I was happy and content. Jaan constantly gave me the most unusual jewelry as presents. I worked as a model for his masterworks. We were always travelling around the world's most special places.

It happened at the Istanbul World Smithing tournament. Jaan had been hammering day and night without a break. Barely had the gold been able to cool a bit when it was put jingling around my wrists, ankles and hips. We reached the final.

Jaan's opponent was a little old man whose origins were unknown to everyone. He was able to hammer out jewelry as fine as mist, but his special trump card was supple and beautifully glimmering golden hair. Copper snakes crafted by the old man twisted their way out of gold chests and coiled round the models' waists and arms. The flute played ever more beautifully and passionately, the drum rumbled some wild and elusive rhythm. Watching this from between the curtains backstage, I suddenly fell into a heavy, restless sleep on my snail sofa. Then Jaan touched my cheek. "Wake up, my dear," he said, pressing onto my head a gold crown on which a hundred seven-metre-long candles were burning. "Our turn!"

I don't remember how it happened, but suddenly Jaan's two strong arms were lying at our feet. The old man smiled sinisterly.

I gave everything else back to Jaan, but I'm holding on to those candles and my wedding ring like some great treasure. I'm not able to forget Jaan. He swore before everyone that it was an accident and his own fault. I escaped a years-long prison sentence and committal to a psychiatric hospital.

Maarja still writes to Jaan to this day. She says he lives in the Kham region of Tibet and has made wings for himself. With the aid of huge shoulder and upper-back muscles he flies around the Himalayas. He's married to a Tibetan beauty and they have a bevy of children. Jaan is the only person in the world who really knows how to fly. Maarja wants us to visit them some time.

When my candles have finally burnt down and my wedding ring no longer sparkles with such a wild dazzle, then perhaps we'll really go.

The Last of the Monogamicans*

It happened in the first quarter of the present century when the Next to Last of the Monogamicans had just gone over to the tribe of the polygamists and had become Back to Front the First of the Polygamicans. After some time, in spite of the polygamist choice he had made, he began to take an interest in his old friend the Last of the Monogamicans.

At first the Last of the Monogamicans wasn't particularly interested in having anything to do with him, but as her own tribe had died out, she decided to restore ties of friendship with her former tribal brother.

The Last of the Monogamicans had adorned herself with care for the coming of Back to Front the First of the Polygamicans. Her fresh body paint glowed, her eagle feathers stood erect. She planned to ritually smoke the peace pipe with Back to Front the First of the Polygamicans. The Polygamican did indeed take a few puffs of their forefathers' poetic pitch and their positivist pipe. But quite soon the Polygamican started to mumble something to himself. The Last of the Monogamicans wanted to know what her friend was mumbling and shifted closer to the Polygamican. But she still couldn't hear properly. She felt that Back to Front the First of the Polygamicans was mumbling

---

* stress on the second and fourth syllables

something about her, or even about himself and her, and was doing this in a... postmodernist way.

Finally the the Last of the Monogamicans' ear was almost against the Polygamican's mouth. Now the Last of the Monogamicans heard what the Polygamican was saying and that excited her very much indeed. It is after all true that women love with their ears. The Last of the Monogamicans turned her face towards Back to Front the First of the Polygamicans and their long, deer-like eyelashes touched and became interwoven.

The Polygamican stroked the Monogamican's hot Amazon shoulders and whispered, "My dear Last of the Monogamicans, come over to polygamy. It's much better here, believe me."

And the Last of the Monogamicans whispered in return, "My dearest Back to Front the First of the Polygamicans, come rather and be again the Next to Last of the Monogamicans beside me. If you wish, you can call youself Back to Front the First of the Monogamicans. Here it is much better, believe me."

Finally, when they had made exes of each other an excess number of times - moving in with each other and then packing their bags and moving out again, it occurred to them early one summer's evening to smoke the peace pipe again. This time it was the Polygamican who offered it to the Last of the Monogamicans. In a run-down yard in the rain of last jasmine blossoms they puffed it wordlessly and the tar-free e-peace pipe smoke filled their deer-like eyes once again with restlessness and joy.

In Athens upon Emajõgi[*]

A fierce struggle over me had been going on all morning. A little goddess with breasts almost reaching to the treetops was on my tail spurring me on. "Think about the fact that you're a woman," she whispered mercilessly. She was the embodiment of lust. Behind her went Apollo, slightly jaded, tapping the goddess of lust from time to time with his walking stick. "Move aside," Apollo hissed through his teeth. "Make way for the educated!". Coming up beside me, he said that he recommended keeping a sober state of mind in my situation. From time to time the Wild Boar-headed Goddess of Fertility attacked the pair of them with her tusks. She swept out of the thicket in the park and forced Apollo and the lustful Goddess of Femininity to retreat. As she came up to me the Wild Boar-headed Goddess rose up on two legs and walked some way with me, supporting me by the elbow. Milk seeped from her eighteen nipples. Her body simply radiated motherhood. Wordlessly she said to me – you are in my power. And that wordless message hit home more strongly than the others' explanations. I held on tightly to her hoof.

Along the riverbank came my betrothed. Times were tense between us. I could already see from afar that he had his own divine escort with him, all of them pushing each other down the riverbank. The

---

[*] *river flowing through the Estonian university town of Tartu*

Seven-headed God of Virile Might and Power was striding beside him. "Always look at women with an eye on how willing they are to submit to you," three heads explained to Jaan, all competing with one another. "If you have to choose between women, choose according to that."

The four remaining heads nodded in agreement.

When the Seven-headed God of Virile Might and Power saw the Wild Boar-headed Goddess of Fertility, he brought forth a tormented groan of frustration from all seven mouths. The Wild Boar-headed beauty accompanying me grunted scornfully and made her eighteen nipples stand erect. From between her sharp tusks she sent an invincibly ironic smile over to the Seven-headed God of Virile Might and Power.

Jaan kissed me and I kissed him back. "Listen, your kiss is like a kiss from my aunt, or even worse, my mother," Jaan declared, giving me a startled look.

"And yours is like something that fell from the mouth of some Ricardo in a Mexican soap," I said, deriding him with pleasure.

The Seven-headed God of Virility and the Wild Boar-headed Goddess of Fertility had got into a scuffle. The ground shook under the thumping of their struggle.

Finally they both fell into Emajõgi, or Mother River, and were carried downstream to where Emajõgi meets Isajõgi, or Father River. Jaan and I looked at each other bewildered, gazing at each other as if through bulletproof glass. Then other gods and goddesses stepped up beside us – Apollo ran over to Jaan, but quickly tired of him, Moon goddess Selene cast a shy, dream-like light over me, Aphrodite stroked me, my speech became soft again and my glance serene and warm. The bulletproof glass between us fell and shattered with a tinkling. Jaan glowed like Shiva. The raw and raging god of night clattered with his wagon across the sky, which was ready for lightning. And Zeus and Hera observed from above how somewhere nearby, where Emajõgi and Isajõgi flow into each other, there was a fierce battle raging over two mortals. Some still unborn human children made a path towards us through the stars and only waited for a signal fire. Where the two rivers meet the Wild Boar-headed Goddess of Fertility and the Seven-headed God of Virile Power climbed out of the riverbank mud again and seven sons hung from the nipples of the fertility goddess. The Seven-headed God of Virile Power had become quiet and drowsy and curled up to sleep in the arms of the Wild Boar-headed beauty in the fatherly and motherly riverbank mud. All the gods and goddesses had forgotten us for a moment or else tired of our company. I suppose they needed a rest and for once, for a few hours before waking, our own will won ground within us. We were full of warmth and friendship for each other, and that is greater than everything else.

The Love Organizer

There was once a certain professional Love Organizer who very much wanted to be employed organizing the Love I felt. "I'm a highly educated worker with a great deal of experience. I've worked on many loves and put things in order. I can see that there's work to be done with your Love as well," he said, trying to convince me.

"My Love doesn't need any organizing," I asserted. "My Love is a freely flowing river, not some sort of thing that needs to be organized."

Packing up his briefcase the Love Organizer eyed me with compassion. "How can anyone be so naive in this day and age!" he muttered and then coughed in a louder voice, "Very well, here is my business card in case you should change your mind."

Outside the snow was blowing. The snowdrifts had completely covered my neighbour's steps. Lying in ambush the walls of snow surrounded the warmth of home, ravenously biting into it wherever they could. I had said my Love was like a river. But what if it freezes over? My Beloved hadn't come home yet and I felt how a thin film of ice was beginning to form at the edges of the river of my Love. Could the Love Organizer find some remedy for this?

The following evening my Beloved still hadn't come and that made my Love hurt. Or did it rather injure that colourless protective layer that, over time, I had cultivated around my Love? On the third day my Beloved phoned. When we finished talking a chilling shiver passed through me. I took a hot water bottle, curled up on the sofa and mechanically dialed the Love Organizer's number.

"Do you know how to keep love from freezing over?" I asked.

"I do," answered the Love Organizer self-confidently.

"Then you're hired." My teeth were chattering.

The Love Organizer's organizing of love was a disappointment to me. As I was stiff with cold, I looked on helplessly while he hired a secretary for himself at my expense and then a detective as well. The detective was to collect information from both my male and female friends about my Beloved's activities. The secretary was to enter the information into the computer. For days the Love Organizer calculated some mystical sums from that. Finally the Love Organizer said that it was time for me to make a bit of an effort as well. He instructed me to dye my hair red, to have a perm and to cut my skirts twenty centimetres shorter. When I told him that I felt even colder than before in those short skirts, he bellowed, "Love yourself and you'll never feel cold!" After that all three of them presented me with huge bills and left, assuring me that they had done everything they could.

When I met my Beloved again a week later, he thought that I had gone mad. He didn't recognise me anymore and neither did I. The river of my love was as frozen as can be. In growing despair I looked at that beautiful river that had once been warm, tempestuous and alluring. Like all fools in love, I had thought that feelings alone are enough. Real feelings should rule out organization.

One day as I sat on the banks of that frozen river and mourned times gone by, I met a man who became my Teacher of Joy.

But on that bleak cold day I had no inkling yet who he was.

Teacher of Joy

A t first the man thought I was a fridge. He looked me over and found that I was a fully functioning fridge. The Teacher of Joy was a strong man and I wasn't a particularly big fridge. He hoisted me up on his shoulder and carried me to his home. I went to work in his kitchen. I kept the Teacher of Joy's red currants well frozen and his containers of milk properly chilled. The Teacher of Joy rejoiced in me and sometimes patted me in passing. At first that was even enough. But soon I began to expect attention and recognition. I wanted to be something more than just a useful appliance. I wanted to be myself again. But how?

The Teacher of Joy was always busy. His work room was directly next to the kitchen and through the door I could often hear how he wept and laughed for joy. But his troubles and joys didn't interest me then.

Perplexed and with some difficulty I moved myself onto my own cable. My droning ceased. By morning the red currants had defrosted and the milk had gone off. The Teacher of Joy examined me for a bit and shifted me off my cable.

The next evening it was the same story. This time he caught me in the act. Being caught out like that made me angry. I exploded and burst into flames. The Teacher of Joy laughed so hard that he had tears in his eyes and cried out "A burning fridge, what an extraordinary sight!"

Finally I had got a bit of attention and recognition from him. That was enough to get my female form back. Feeling gratified I stood in the light blue flames over the fridge and looked angrily at the Teacher of Joy.

My grievously difficult studies in joy had begun.

The Surrealist's Daughter

The first time I went to visit the Surrealist's daughter, I was bitten by the Surrealist's dog. He bit me in the thigh through the mesh gate. "A really surrealistic wound," I thought, feeling my leg. It didn't really hurt, but it was great to see how the Surrealist's daughter and her mother came running with a bottle of iodine and adhesive bandages, how they knelt down in front of me to treat my wound. The Surrealist's daughter looked at me with big, startled, slightly guilty eyes. I smiled at her but she didn't smile back.

The next time we met was several years later. It happened to be St George's Night and it was the first time that I saw the Surrealist's daughter completely naked. She stepped in suddenly through the door of the smoke sauna and in the darkness I didn't immediately realize who this woman was. She sat down next to me on the sooty bench and we didn't look at each other. Only later, when I saw one of her strange confirmation dresses and her patterned stockings hanging over a beam in the sauna's front room did I realize who I was having a sauna with.

The third time I met the Surrealist's daughter, I talked all sorts of rubbish. I told her that I had been dreaming only of a woman like her all my life. I smiled at her again and repeated her name several times. In all seriousness. But the Surrealist's daughter turned into a black stork and sat instead on the shoulder of one of my friends. She rubbed her long neck against my friend's cheek. I saw my friend straining not to turn into a frog and he finally managed it, turning into a punk rocker instead. The punk rocker took the Surrealist's daughter who had turned into a black stork to be his driver. "I'd like to go to Hiiumaa island now," the punk rocker said and the black stork straightaway sat down behind the wheel. I watched for some time as they drove away. Then I went off to send some emails and went to bed. That night I dreamed that I was flying to who knows where in the dark of night on the back of a black stork that was croaking sadly. My friend later told me that in Hiiumaa he hadn't been able to resist the temptation and had gone behind a lilac bush with a blonde blue-eyed punk rocker to drink beer. At the same time the black stork was supposed to fill the tank and get some synthetic motor oil, mosquito repellant and something to eat. But when the punk rocker went back to the black stork in the hotel room, none of this had been done. The stork had meanwhile turned back into the Surrealist's daughter. She lay in her thin white dress on the red carpet and wept.

My friend said that from that moment on he didn't know whether to take it or leave it. He thrashed about for a long time in some nameless and confused identity crisis and finally decided that the stork was all right as far as it goes – but the weeping Surrealist's daughter was just too much.

The fourth time I saw the Surrealist's daughter, she was sitting on a tree and combing her long silky hair. I looked up at her and said that she was so beautiful. I smiled and she smiled back at me. I said that to my mind she was very, very beautiful. I added quite loudly, to be sure that she heard me, that I had always wanted just her sort of woman. I thought about what else I could say. I said that of course I had wanted just such a mother for my children as well. I got into quite a flow with my words. When I looked up again at her in the tree, she wasn't there any more. She had fallen down and broken her rib. When I drove her to the emergency department, she wept inconsolably and said, "Please don't say such things to me. It's more than I can bear". And yet straight after that she begged, with tears in her eyes, "Say some more, please".

I continued saying things of that very nature to her the entire time. I let my fantasy flow freely. Although I saw that she was barely able to prepare a meal, that she dropped plates, used too much salt, burned the potatoes, I told her that I would like her to be the mistress of my farm, that I admired her ability to look after things and create beauty all around her. I smiled, for from the corner of my eye I saw the Surrealist's daughter's dusty bookshelves, unwashed windows and other suchlike things. Thereupon she kissed me, as if in passing, yet more passionately than I had ever been kissed by any woman before that, and then she suddenly asked me to go away. She said she needed to get up in the middle of the night and perform.

Perform... the Surrealist's daughter knew how to do that. After all, she worked in a cabaret. Her job was frying the hearts and other body parts of her male audience over a low flame. She did that with her dancing and of course with her ability to transform herself. She was a woman of many faces and many bodies.

Next time I told the Surrealist's daughter about my women. I told her about them seemingly by the way while we were driving around Egypt in a rented jeep. I had invited her on the trip with me. I wanted to completely entangle her mind with tales of my former and present women and then propose marriage to her. It was so good with her, I thought, why shouldn't we go even further.

But entangling the mind of the Surrealist's daughter had other much more serious consequences than I could imagine. Between a sphinx and a pyramid in the desert, the Surrealist's daughter turned into a fire-spouting dragon that had wound itself around a trembling maiden dressed in white. The maiden looked exactly like the Surrealist's daughter, only half her age. The dragon sent caustic tongues of fire in my direction which were very painful indeed. The maiden looked on with an air of suffering and I wondered with a feeling of revulsion why I should even bother fussing with this Surrealist's daughter and all her conjurings. Of course I left her. And then I left her again. But our paths kept crossing, for in the course of time we had become friends.

One bright, warm night when she had just come from performing and her body was hot and smelled of frying hearts, we met by chance on the street and went up the hill to look at the moon. I just couldn't help myself and again brought up the subject of marriage while at the same time making her jealous with tales of my other women. "Yes, I've had countless numbers of them, in the first years I tried to keep a tally of them, but now it's all in a hopeless muddle," I said, ostensibly by the bye. "But you're different, with you I almost want to... Yes, with you and only you." I called her again several times by her name. In all seriousness. "And yet I'm afraid of that," I continued. "Sometimes I'm gripped by panic when I think that I might have to be with someone for the rest of my life and be faithful to her."

I should have known I was playing with fire. Again the dragon was standing before me and the maiden was looking at me with her beautiful, trembling eyes. First the dragon bit a chunk out of my thigh. Then it ripped out one of my ribs and bit it in half. The maiden was still looking at me gravely and beseechingly, and neither the full moon nor she, nor even the black stork that had suddenly landed on a blossoming white lilac bush could be of any help to me. Behind the maiden stood the cabaret dancer rolling her hips and stroking her breasts. It fried my heart and not only that. Then the dragon turned its seven heads towards me and got ready to tear me apart once and for all and then set me alight.

For some reason I wasn't able to run away, for the maiden's innocent, beseeching gaze and the cabaret dancer's rolling hips held me fixed to the spot. Blood flowed from my thigh and my side and the dragon mocked me haughtily. I thought it would be good to fall asleep at that very moment, for death wouldn't be so terrible coming in sleep. I closed my eyes. At that moment I freed myself from the spell cast by the cabaret dancer and the eyes of that grave young maiden. I turned into St George on his white horse, a sword as long as a ship's mast grew in my hand. I hewed the dragon. Or did I hew the Surrealist's daughter? In any case, when every last one of the heads was off, we were dripping with blood. Me, the maiden, the white horse, the black stork, the cabaret dancer, the lilac bush and even the moon – we were all blood-red. And to put an end to all this hocus-pocus I rode home to my farm with them, washed them clean and put them to bed. When the Surrealist's daughter woke in the morning, she was again all of a piece, she still had the moon in her arms and she smelt of lilac. She told me that she had become pregnant from the blood of her own dragon and we would straightaway be having two pairs of three-headed twins who would all look exactly like me.

The Off-Roader's Daughter

When I went for a walk with our three-headed twins, I must have been the strangest and happiest father that this middling village-sized capital of a small country had ever seen. Our twins were just simply wonderfully dear. And I had begun to like the Surrealist's daughter so much that from time to time I simply had to feel a certain interest for the Off-Roader's daughter in order to keep my freedom, which was worth gold to me.

Every time I phoned her she was at the hairdresser's, pedicurist's or being depilated. Every time I went to visit her she was in those same places. Whereupon I usually went for a swim in the sea, naked. There I felt free as well and imagined that I would be able to cool down and in my heart take a bit of distance to the Surrealist's daughter's love. But it generally didn't work out that way – she and our three-headed children danced and grew in my changing heart. I felt that I would need a lifetime to get as close to them as I wanted to. And the road seemed sweet and gnawed with magic power at the fetters of freedom that I had intended to bind myself with for the rest of my life.

One night, coming back from swimming, the Off-Roader's daughter stood on the shore, depilated, pedicured, with intoxicatingly scented curls. She grabbed my clothes from the stone and ran off. Me in pursuit. I soon caught up with her and shook her angrily. Women think they can do whatever they want. I was amazed that the Off-Roader's daughter seemed to be expecting that. She apparently enjoyed being shaken.

"Shake me some more!"she pleaded.

"No, I won't!" I said.

But I kept shaking her. I wanted to see if she would turn into something or someone. But she remained the depilated Off-Roader's daughter who liked being shaken.

"Why do you so enjoy being shaken?" I asked when I had already shaken her several times with all my might.

"It makes me feel I'm something more than a depilated husk. When everything in me shakes, I'm afraid of losing what is shaking. And then the one that's afraid is me after all" answered the Off-Roader's daughter.

I kept shaking her. She groaned.

And then it happened. Depilation, pedicure and everything else fell off onto the ground. Facing me stood small off-roader-shaped fear itself. The fear was very clean, shining and fast. Before I was able to stroke it sympathetically it accelerated and took off like the wind towards the horizon. That scream of fear smelling of petrol reverberated in my ears for a long time. I realised that with the Off-Roader's daughter, shaking was not the right tactic. I didn't wish to do it anymore, nor did I get a chance to, for the Off-Roader's daughter spent the rest of her life in the very same places as before.

Partly Good

After that I looked for the Surrealist's daughter and our three-headed twins everywhere. They weren't at home, in the office, in the atelier, at the riverside or any of the secret places I was partly aware of. It was a clear summery day. Sand martins circled over the rooftops. A sticky silence flowed into my ears. I poured music into my ears, the voices of friends, the rumble of cars, the ringing of phones and more friends' voices, but nothing helped. The sticky hot silence wrapped itself around my heart. I set off towards my partly punk-rock friend, on whose shoulder the black stork of the Surrealist's daughter had once sat.

We chatted. But I didn't hear him any more. His voice suddenly reminded me of the black stork's woeful croaking and this became ever weaker and more distant until it finally faded away completely. We sat on my friend's step under a bush that smelled of something or other and we drank something. I couldn't taste anything. But I carried on drinking. Yet some sensations flowed over me nevertheless – for a moment I sensed the sour-sweet smell streaming from the bush's pink blossoms, the bitter taste of the drink, my friend's voice, the stork's croaking and the stabbing pain of loss. Then they all disappeared again.

I lingered in that partly soundless, tasteless, scentless state for quite some time. Now and again I took some sensual girl friend out dancing and to warm my bed. It was good. But that "good" was fleeting in a mad way. To tell the truth it was partly good. And for some reason I didn't feel any better.

When after a long time I heard of the Surrealist's daughter again, she was just getting divorced from the Off-Roader. The Off-Roader's daughter had been her stepchild and was now clinging very strongly to her stepmother. She followed the Surrealist's daughter everywhere, played with our three-headed twins and looked up to her stepmother with adoring eyes. Suddenly I realized that this young girl wasn't the Off-Roader's daughter anymore. Now she was the stepdaughter of the Surrealist's daughter. The Surrealist's daughter treated her tenderly and with respect. From time to time they must have even gone to those same places. But the one that I wanted to shake now was the Surrealist's daughter.

Yet I didn't shake her. There was some sort of ring of brightness around her that even from a distance shook my wish to shake her.

The Beekeeper's Stepdaughter

In the meantime the Surrealist's daughter had adopted another father for herself. That father was a beekeeper. Because of that from time to time the Surrealist's daughter became the Beekeeper's stepdaughter. At those times she gave very surrealistic, buzzing parties at her atelier. When I went there one evening, a swarm of male bees was buzzing around the Beekeeper's stepdaughter. The Surrealist's daughter no longer had her ring of brightness. In its place was... mmm... I don't even know what. When I tried to approach her, I turned into one of those male bees myself. The Beekeeper's stepdaughter apparently enjoyed that delightful buzzing and male attention. She allowed one particularly big and stocky male bee to sit on the blossom of her shoulder. Yes, her shoulder had truly blossomed and was pollinating tantalisingly. I made myself some tea and sat on the other shoulder of the Beekeeper's stepdaughter, but for some reason that one didn't blossom.

The big, stocky male bee grew even bigger from the attentions of the Beekeeper's stepdaughter and her shoulder blossomed more and more with each moment.

Listening to their honeyed talk was at first somehow painful and embarrassing to me. I wasn't at all a honey sort of man myself and had never been able to talk that way. Simply being boisterous had always seemed easier and grander. I tried being a bit boisterous with the

Beekeeper's stepdaughter, but she didn't get into the swing of it at all, but kept on listening entranced to the stocky male bee.

"How can you listen to such sweet rubbish," I buzzed crossly into the ear of the Beekeeper's stepdaughter. Supremely sweet and intoxicating pollen was seeping from the unattainable blossom of her shoulder.

The Beekeeper's daughter didn't even hear me. I noted with alarm that all the compliments that male was paying her became true on the spot.

"Your eyes are like the sea rippling lightly on a sunny morning," the man said flatteringly Straightaway that very same sea rippled in the eyes of the Beekeeper's stepdaughter.

"But deep in your fathomless eyes are unimagined oceans," the stocky fellow announced. At that very moment we saw the open expanse of the ocean in the deep gaze of the Beekeeper's stepdaughter.

I stared at her, utterly entranced. Was this really the same woman I had once...? That ocean painfully reminded me again of the Surrealist's daughter. Sitting on the shoulder of the Beekeeper's stepdaughter, I had almost forgotten her.

Soon that thriving male bee had to go to a meeting. He got into his Mercedes and buzzed off towards the horizon.

The Beekeeper's stepdaughter slowly began to turn back into the Surrealist's daughter, though her shoulder continued blossoming and she went round like that for several days. And the joyful sea and fathomless ocean still looked out from her eyes. She was again enveloped in a ring of brightness that collided with a rumbling against my wish to be boisterous. Her motherly peace struck again like lightning into my desire to shake her.

Full Circle

I never did get the Surrealist's daughter any more. And she didn't get me. Our lives ran parallel to one another and never crossed again. Yet we did bump into each other once on the street. We smiled exactly the same smile at each other at the same moment. Then we asked each other "How are you?" at exactly the same time. On that our eyes filled at the same time with exactly the same sort of tears and then we smiled at each other again. At exactly the same time.

The Surrealist's dog had, in the meantime, been put into a separate enclosure. He'll never bite anyone again through the gate, I thought. But on my thigh there was still a scar left by the Surrealist's dog and the bite of the Surrealist's daughter's dragon. Perhaps this little scar was a sign that deep down I am still her lover. And she mine. Some ties simply last a whole lifetime. No matter who we become.

Our three-headed twins dealt with completely different matters in life than the Surrealist's daughter and I did. They weren't as attention-seeking as we were. They learnt to be completely inconspicuous and in that way really found their real selves along with deep love and peace of mind.

The Princely Paintbrush and the Princess

Recently a certain Princely Paintbrush started liking me again. He came every evening in his red Passat and stood before me, the wish to paint plain to see in his eyes. I splashed him with water just for the fun of it. I smiled at him in a princessly sort of way. The Paintbrush liked that. He delicately touched my white skin, which immediately became even whiter and silkier. I became ever more Princess-like. He painted me and shaped me and the Princely Paintbrush particularly liked this shaping.

But suddenly he changed his mind and painted me as a wicked queen who had disguised herself as an old hag and had come to sell an apple to a snow-white Princess. The Princess took a big bite out of the red side of the apple I had given her. And the Paintbrush made that half of the apple particularly red. He skillfully coloured the glass coffin and took care that the Princess's cheeks in that coffin would still be as red as his own Passat.

Then suddenly he thought again and painted me as an apple. Utterly an apple. I was put on sale at a market and I was beautiful, fresh and tempting. Who was going to buy me? Who was going to notice me and know how to appreciate me? The Princely Paintbrush waited. Then he painted himself in the shape of a man and came to buy me. He got me all to himself. He bit into my juicy fruit flesh. But I got stuck in his throat. Apparently I wasn't poisonous, but perhaps just too big a piece for him. He drew a glass coffin for himself. Then he lay down in it with the piece of me stuck in his throat.

The Paintbrush and the Princess were carried in their glass coffins to one and the same hill on the outskirts of the city. They lay there at the edge of the mystery of life and death and looked up at the starry August sky. The Princess was the first to awaken. The apple's poison in her throat lost all its effect the moment it dawned on her that she was dealing with a very stereotypical situation. She spit out the piece of apple, stepped out of the glass coffin straight over to the Paintbrush and kissed him tenderly on the lips. This made the Paintbrush swallow so voraciously that he gulped that big chunk of me down.

Of course the Princely Paintbrush kissed the Princess in return and already wanted to start painting and shaping once again.

The Dried Apricots
of My Six Former Husbands

My six former husbands all had big juicy apricots. Lots of people would have wanted to taste them, but I was the only one who got near them. Yesterday I went again to the dark attic room where I keep them. The last apricot I took up there still hasn't really dried. It's moist and its surface feels velvety and warm. I feel at one and the same time both proud and ashamed of my frightening collection. This small apricot here which has dried nearly black belonged to my first husband. Every so often he loved to stress what a great swine he was. I was still very young and waited in fear all the time for when he would become a swine. But he didn't. Before that could happen the idea of my collection came to me and I snatched his apricot away.

My second husband really was a swine, but he never admitted it himself. His apricot is this angular and slightly purple fruit here. Actually it's reminiscent of a plum.

My third husband was the best of them all. On the night I carried away the most beautiful among his half-dozen apricots I spilt bitter tears. I felt that I really shouldn't have snatched that particular fruit. But until now the strongest of all my feelings has proven to be my passion for collecting.

My fourth husband was a collector just like me. We understood each other with half a word and promised to leave each other's treasures in peace. I broke the vow. I made a decisive grab for his apricot just as he was stretching his hand out for my stamens. I know that sooner or later he would have robbed me naked. His apricot still smells sweet to this day. It smells of victory that became mine by a razor's breadth.

My fifth husband was a professor at the Academy of Forgettings. I was his favourite student. I have no memory of the day our relationship began. I have no memory of days and nights spent together – not a single word, scent or touch. I don't even remember how his apricot finally got here. But just now, as I stroke the rough skin of this dried out fruit, I think that I probably didn't particularly love him. And I left my studies in forgettings unfinished just before defending my doctoral thesis. Existence becomes somehow desolate if you can't remember anything at all anymore. I only know that we were together for a whole year. A whole year of my life, my youth! Oh, how I would like to snatch back the cycle of that year, that energy and dedication that was in me.

And this sixth drying apricot here belonged to the man of my dreams. No wonder then that in this worldly life everything went as it did. But still a pity, a great pity, that he didn't see through me either. I did after all give him a vital hint. I told him that I only reveal myself on one short summer's night. He really came to see how I opened up. I very much hoped he would notice what I hide so jealously for the rest of the year. But he, he still only saw my stamens, saw in me the woman of his dreams. And what are you going to do with someone like that?

Stranger

One day when my heart was sorely aching over some old worry and I wandered aimlessly along the rainy streets of my favourite summer resort town, I met that peculiar man again. Just like the last time, he had a thermos of sweet black tea with him. We sat on a bench at the seaside and the edges of our umbrellas touched. I felt how a happy tremor ran up my spine and my heart suddenly filled with a feeling of great friendship.

How is it that again and again I run into this man who hasn't played for 55,000 years? Maybe he complements my own tragically playful nature very well. In any case I don't want anything to come of it for him with me. Maybe he's the very one I'll show my apricot collection to one day. Maybe some time I'll tell him about this old worry that is just now making my heart ache so. But already he takes a last sip of his cloyingly sweet tea, gets up, tips his hat, and leaves. I watch him moving off along the way lined with leafless linden trees. With slow, measured stride he steps over the muddy leaves that will soon decay into soil.

Lena of the Drifting Isle

1

It happened years later. I showed Oskar – that was the man's name – my collection. He introduced me to his wife Lena. We went to a café together. We climbed up the old-fashioned wooden stairs to the open terrace on the third floor. Lena was beautiful in her nakedness. She didn't have a scrap of clothing on her, nor did she have any skin, flesh or blood. She was a skeleton.

We sat on high velvet upholstered chairs. I ordered a cappucino. I looked at Lena. There was still a bit of white sand in the hollow of her skull. Her hand lay on the table. Oskar placed the big warm palm of his own hand lovingly over Lena's delicate knuckles. A sensitive tremor passed through her ribcage. Her ribs expanded as she breathed in and she shifted herself closer to Oskar.

We spoke Italian to make it easier for Lena to understand us. She's a born Latin.

"What would you like, my dear?"

"Just water, please," Lena said. Her voice was soft and warm. I spoke to Lena and Oskar about the bird that is teaching me its language. It comes onto a branch of an old pear tree in my garden every evening. I sit there under the tree in a wicker chair on the banks of a river flowing through our garden and write the first bird language grammar. It's a strange, illogical system where nearly everything is founded on emotion.

Lena nodded and mentioned that she had once known a bird as well. "I'll tell you about it another time," she said with a smile.

Lena and Oskar were great listeners. They were attentive and asked informed questions that were interesting to answer.

Finally I asked Lena about her life. She told me that she had been born on the Isle of Flying Sand. This had once been like any other island, but one fine day before Lena's birth it had torn itself free from the ocean floor. It became a small and restless floating island meandering about in the expanse of the ocean. The sand on this island also drifted around from one dune to another, from one swirling eddy of sand to another. In the course of time the people adapted and those who didn't move away learnt to dance with the sand. "We even slept flitting back and forth," she told me. Her voice was dreamy and bright.

Lena took a sip of her lemon water and I saw how it trickled down along her beautiful white bones. Oskar put his arm around Lena and gently stroked her wet backbone. Lena shifted even closer to Oskar.

"Yet one day the island fell apart," Oskar continued, "and Lena's family moved to a big coral country. It was the sort of country where money was never used."

"Did they pay with coral?" I asked with interest.

"No, they didn't," Oskar explained. "Time was regarded as the most valuable thing in that country. Those who worked simply got more time added on..."

"Mmm... delightful..." I took a last sip of the cream foam on my coffee and dreamt of a job in a country like that.

Oskar arranged a big mohair shawl around Lena's shoulders.

We went home through parks and along tree-lined paths. They lived in the very same garden-suburb of wooden houses as I did. Stars flashed, flying from one bottomless depth to another in the sky. The lone tusk of the new moon had tumbled over into the night clouds when we said good-bye at Lena's and Oskar's gate under an old wild damson tree.

I squeezed Lena's hand warmly.

"See you."

"Arrivederci!"

2

Lena continued her story a few weeks later as we sat together in my attic room. It was the first time I had invited Lena to visit me. She sat in my armchair on soft cushions, onto which I had embroidered all sorts of wondrous many-coloured birds, flowers and dancing children. Her finger bones stroked my needlework as she went on, reminiscing slowly.

"We settled down to live in that coral country in a seaside tower. It had once been a grand castle, but now all that remained were two towers. The castle had once belonged to a raven king, but now only his daughter lived there – the young Raven Princess. Her other castle tower stood empty and she kindly allowed us to settle in there."

"We lived there quite pleasantly for half a thousand years," Lena said, continuing her tale. "I worked in the nearby sand castle as a dancer and tamed a herd of small playful ringed seals at the Circus of Dreams. My father had a dune-rose nursery at the seashore. On Sundays I was a gardener there. One day I was just watering a rose bush the size of a chestnut tree that had really luxuriant blossoms when a handsome prince came riding up to me on the back of a golden cheetah. He was the heir to the throne of a faraway desert realm and wanted to buy our most expensive Rambling Magic Flowers. I sold him a wondrously beautiful sort. As he paid he looked into my eyes very meaningfully and when our fingers touched, the dark tremor of first love passed through me. The time granted by the prince tasted sweet and seemed endlessly long."

I had to break the thread of Lena's tale, as it was eight o' clock and my bird was waiting for me on the pear tree branch. I put the half-finished bird language grammar under my arm and walked with Lena as far as the garden gate. We agreed to meet again soon.

3

The following week we sat on the pale pink carpet in my attic room and bored holes into grains of sand using Lena's wonder-needle. We made long, fragile bead necklaces of them. It was the latest fashion in our town. Lena was the only one who knew how to make such necklaces. My wardrobe had changed entirely during our brief acquaintance. Lena taught me to wear fescue-green and nut-coloured dresses. She superbly matched up the most diverse materials. She liked to plait my long, rush-coloured hair. She taught me to look at my figure in my shadow. This was much better than self-critical superficial twirling in front of a mirror. I wore two long ribbons in my hair that reached down to my knees. They were so richly decorated that there was no need for any other adornments. Lena said that she'd learnt this trick 1600 years ago from a beauty who was as fine as mist. Lena taught me the simple truth that as long as you have flesh on your bones you're beautiful. Then adorn yourself only as much as you like and feel joy and pride in your beauty. Later, yes later, an altogether different esthetic begins. Lena easily drilled holes into grains of sand and I strung them on thread. I asked Lena to continue telling me her life story.

"I liked the man on the cheetah very much," Lena said. "He came every Sunday and bought up our most beautiful flowers. I waited for him eagerly. I hoped that he only came to buy our flowers because of me." Lena fell silent for a while.

"Finally the one day in the year was at hand when the men in that coral realm went to ask for the hand of their beloved in marriage. That day was known as Friday of Restless Love," Lena recalled. "Young men wove wreaths of the Climbing Roses of Sorrowing Youth and presented them to their chosen ones, who stood waiting at the windows of their homes. The Prince had bought a big bunch of these promised flowers from me the night before. I adorned myself in the morning sunlight. I stood at my window and waited. I waited and waited, my eyes fixed on the towering crags in the distance – is the cheetah's yellow muzzle not flashing between them yet, is my Prince not coming yet?

Then he appeared. I jumped for joy. He had a wedding wreath in his hand, his black hair danced in the wind. Soon-soon he'll be under my window, soon he'll throw the wreath to me and stretch out his hand. I'll run down the spiral staircase and he'll ask, "Will you come and be my wife, Lena of the Drifting Isle?" I'll nod and exude a fragrance. I'm nearly all fragrance, the intoxicating sweet fragrance of the wreath of the Climbing Roses of Sorrowing Youth. I'll jump behind him onto the back of the of the cheetah and we'll speed off together to his kingdom, where all the remaining moments of my life beside him will be as beautiful as a dream.

Suddenly I stiffen into a pillar of salt. The Prince rides his cheetah to the castle tower where the Raven Princess lives. I stretch out of the window and see how the Princess catches the wreath and puts it on her head to fasten her veil. She comes down the spiral staircase and reaches out to the Prince with her coal-black wing. Already they are on the back of the cheetah speeding off in a flurry. But still, long-long after the Raven Princess and the Prince have disappeared beyond the coral crags stretching out on the horizon, the Raven Princess's long bridal veil is still trailing behind them down the stairs. It is made of some particularly fine tulle on which are growing – shadowy indeed are the paths of hope! – my most beautiful flowers, all the ones the Prince had bought from me."

Lena sighs and smiles sadly for a moment. And we continue working for a while in silence.

4

In the evening I told this story to my bird. It nodded ardently and picked up the thread of the story where I had left off.

"That prince was a well-known heartbreaker," it told me. "My grandmother was in love with him too when she was young. She sat on a tree and wept as she watched the prince and his bride gallop off on the cheetah's back to their desert castle. My grandmother was a beautiful bird but she wasn't of high birth and the Prince didn't even look at her. Every day my grandmother had to feed the cheetah and deliver the Prince's letters. From the time the Prince brought the Raven Princess into the house, my granny could do nothing but weep. She did everything and saw to everything just as before, but now big painful tears rolled from her eyes all the time. The Prince quite liked that in the beginning. He loved to boast that the Weeping Bird worked in his castle. Later he tired of it and washed his hands in my grandmother's tears and then dried them in soft bird feathers. This made my grandmother weep even more. A stream sprang from her tears, flowed down from the castle window, murmured long between the sandy hills of the desert realm, flowed to the the steep brink of the plateau which was at the same time the border of the desert realm, gathered there into a great river and plunged down the precipice as a waterfall. There below began dense thickets, vast coverts, wide impenetrable woodlands. It was a land where devourers of hope lived, and it was through these savage places that my grandmother's river of tears now crawled. It swelled ever greater and greater and from thicket to thicket, wasteland to wasteland, it thrashed about restlessly in search of a bed to flow in.

No one knew where this river with its clear water sprang from. The people of the desert realm quenched their eternal thirst in it. The devourers of hope dipped their newborn children into it. But they put their departed onto bulrush rafts, set them aflame and pushed them downstream.

Downstream came new expanses. The realm of the rich came, the realm of the foolish ape-people who sawed the branch they were sitting on, then came the United Kingdom of Seven Birds' Realms, after that came the realm of traitors and the realm where everyone was renowned. Further on came apparently endless flatlands and high, snowy mountainous lands before the river reached the immense Sea of Joy.

One day my grandmother became so sad in the Prince's desert castle that she pressed her wings across her breast, jumped into the river of her very own tears and tried to drown herself. But the salty river of tears held her on the suface and carried her on and on ever nearer to that sea, whose call and whisper she felt in the bend of her wings. Lena of the Drifting Isle jumped into that river too, as did the Raven Princess and the cheetah – even she was madly in love with her Prince. In the end the Prince himself jumped in. But where and when they reached the riverbank or whether any of them ever made it as far as the Sea of Joy, I don't know.

It is said that my granny fell into her final slumber that very same spring when my mother learnt to fly. But before that my grandmother showed my mother the way. And I am proceeding the very same way downstream along the river of my granny's tears of youth. And the fact that now for a change I've made a nest in this little town only signifies a snug, fleeting sojourn before a new journey, before continuing the great adventure..."

I'd already known some time before that my bird loved to inflate its words, but even so, my soul became tender and restless from listening to this fairy tale. I left the tenth chapter of my bird language grammar unfinished and went for a walk in my garden along the riverbank. It occurred to me that old folk call this river the River of Weeping and that every drop of water in this river really is as salty as tears.

Gold Key

Now that I have completely mastered bird language and the grammar I authored is already in its fifteenth printing, I've nearly forgotten my apricot collection. Only very rarely indeed on some rainy autumn night do I remember it. Then I take my little gold key from its hook and go up the attic stairs to that familiar door. I've strictly forbidden my husband to open the door. "You can go into every room in our house, but please keep away from my little attic chamber," I've told him firmly. Fortunately, my husband isn't a particularly curious person and he hasn't stumbled upon my collection yet. He has his own collections too that are hidden behind all sorts of passwords.

But why am I hiding this fruit from my husband at all, I've wondered while looking at my collection. Probably because my husband is short-sighted and in addition to that is prone to flights of fantasy. He could easily mistake those apricots for something completely different. One person doesn't even have skin or flesh, another has a wife who is a skeleton and he himself hasn't played in 55,000 years, a third cries a whole riverful of tears, a fourth breaks hearts like flowers, a fifth has no sense of curiosity at all, a sixth merely has a few apricots...

I still haven't told my husband what will happen if one day he should misuse my gold key.

But one morning, when I prepared a sweet apricot compote for him and he complained that the taste of some of the apricots was nothing special, I told him angrily that I don't like men who moan about food and make such a fuss about every little bit of fruit. He apologised and after that there were no more clashes between us.

In the end we all have to swallow the collections of our husbands and wives. Even if we pretend that we're not the slightest bit interested.

Four Skaters

Four skaters swept along the moonlit snow. They all held one another's hands. They were all one another's grand-aunts and at the same time fathers-in-law as well. And still they were so hellishly young. That knowledge gave them even more momentum.

It had been a sparkling sunny day. Now that brightness was fading. From a distance the four skaters were barely discernible. In truth, they couldn't be seen at all. Only one hoary old soul barely out of childhood climbing up a rope ladder to the heavens looked down squinting for a moment and noticed them.

A slender squirrel took off her coat and stepped into the beauty salon. She requested a bit of massage. And a bit of delicate, natural midday make-up. She went out into the street. It was suddenly so hot. She folded her coat over her arm. The squirrel was slim, lithe, fragile, naked now, her big eyes marvelling at the fading brightness of that early spring day. All the men who saw her fell utterly in love with her. They followed at her heels, forgetting their own faithful human wives who were now only suitable as friends. The squirrel defeated and conquered them all without even realizing it herself.

The librarian Juuli saw from the window that her husband was also following the squirrel girl as if in a dream. She grabbed her grey coat and ran out into the street. Every step she took made a piercing sound, as if she were walking along a piano keyboard. The music made by her feet was so beautiful and sad that everyone who heard it began to weep. There are always people in the world who long to weep. They followed Juuli and wept, especially when Juuli tried to call to her husband, for that sounded like the most beautiful song.

"Where are you going?" Juuli called." For the sake of our children Kevin and Hanna-Maria, come back....!"

The long procession following the delicate squirrel-woman headed down towards the river. The long procession following Juuli also headed down towards the river. The evening sun shimmered warmly against the bare, frosty poplar trunks.

The hoary old soul barely out of childhood on the ladder to the heavens made the ladder start swaying. More, more momentum! Now he was sweeping back and forth over the town, holding on to a rung of the ladder first with one hand, then the other. The last rays of the sun danced in and out of his squinting eyes.

A big crowd had gathered outside the Orthodox Church. The desire for holy communion had come upon them, all at the same time. "Now, at night?" wondered the sexton. The hungry, thirsty crowd forced its way past him into the church and knelt before the altar. They filled the whole church. And they filled the whole churchyard.

The priest of not this but another church was at that moment eating his evening meal at a Georgian restaurant together with his lover. But his lover was the priest of that very church where the whole of the congregation had suddenly been overcome by a hunger for receiving grace. She was the first female Orthodox priest on the planet and, as she was the first, she still didn't know very well how things went. Suddenly her dearest, the priest of that other church, rushed off in pursuit of the squirrel-girl and she received a phone call at the very same moment requesting her to come to the church where the congregation was waiting for her. She looked at the pile of chewed lamb ribs on the table in front of her. She wiped the fat off her lips, looked doubtfully at her companion floating away down the darkening street lined with chestnut trees, stretching his hand out like someone who was moonstruck, towards the delicate movements of the squirrel's body.

She went unwillingly against the flow to where the congregation was waiting for her. "Grace," sang the congregation as if with one voice. "Not bread nor wine nor the word of God, but grace is what we all want today. Grace!!!" It sounded like snarling. It sounded like growling.

The crowd hungering for grace made way for their priestess. But before she reached the altar they ate her. The most merciless and gluttonous people have always been those hungering for grace. But where the priestess was eaten another immediately appeared in her place. The crowd fell upon her as well. Again another grew in her place. So there was a great eating and drinking there, a demanding and casting away of grace.

The four young skaters who were all great-aunts and at the same time fathers-in-law to one another came speeding along the river. Unseen they skated through the mass of people. They wrenched the woman priest away from the crowd that was hungering for grace and carried her far away. Of the evening sun only a purple glimmer was left on the ice.

Everything was slowly buried in the dark and defenceless spring night. The squirrel-girl put her coat on and slipped into the hollow of a tree to sleep. Juuli got her husband back. Those who wanted to had been able to cry. The hoary old soul barely out of childhood stopped the ladder swinging and climbed slowly towards heaven. Only the restless mob still hungering for grace blathered on, making a racket in the street around the church well into the middle of the night.

Cushions

I t once so happened that I married a man who loved to talk as much and listen as little as I did. At first everything seemed to be ideal. I never noticed we were trying to talk over each other. I felt that he was a good listener. Every time I thought of something particularly clever and looked over at him he was just moving his lips. Later my doctor explained to me that I had already become completely deaf by then. That was a terrible day. I realised that whenever I related my tales to my husband, he was relating his to me at the same time. And neither of us heard what the other was saying, for my husband was deaf too. It was a particular kind of deafness – we were able to distinguish all the other sounds in the world, but we were totally deaf to each other's voice.

But we very much loved to talk. And we very much loved each other.

In spite of that it became necessary to put an end to such pointless storytelling. One evening, when we were caught up in the flow of talk, the same thought occurred to both of us. We suddenly pressed cushions between each other's jaws.

It was an unaccustomed feeling. Neither of us could move our mouth for several long seconds. Then we swallowed the cushions down at the same time. We kept pressing more and yet more cushions into each other's mouth and again and again swallowed them down. It was a maddening situation. Although neither of us could hear the other, at the end of the day one of us should have shut up and concentrated on the other's stories for appearance's sake, if for nothing else.

The last two cushions got stuck between our jaws. All of a sudden we were utterly full of cushions.

There was a giant in our village who had won the hand of a dragon bride. They were quite poor and one day they simply took us to be their pillows. The young dragon bride rested her head on me and the giant rested his on my husband. We lay side by side at the head of their bed and felt with our entire bodies the enamoured breathing of those two primeval beings.

Dragon's Diary

I've already seen one thing and another, even a third and a fourth in this world, but wherever I've searched, wherever I've crept, I haven't found sex.

What sort of thing is this sex that everyone talks about and falls silent about? I don't understand.

Now I'm married to this Giant here. Every evening he puts his heavy hands around me. He cuddles me and caresses me. Tenderly kisses my three mouths and three necks. I become more and more heated from this until I start spouting flames and then gradually cool down, like lava that has flowed into a cold spring. Our bed is full of smoke and in the hiss of cooling down I feel the beating of his big heart under my claws. Thump-thump-thump-thump...

But what part of all this – the beginning, the end, the middle, or all of it together – is sex, that I don't know.

This morning I asked my husband and he answered with a laugh that sex is when I once lost my tail under our blanket and he helped me to find it.

Depressing. How is that supposed to happen again? You can't consciously lose your tail under the blanket. That can only happen by chance. And what might also happen by chance is that I will never chance upon it again. Best to forget it altogether. The word is already getting on my nerves. Sex. Sounds like a trap being sprung. Who invented this mysterious trap anyway? Clack. And all at once it captures your most beautiful moments. It's aggravating and intrusive. It's a third party when you want to be alone, just the two of you. I hope I manage to forget it.

I said that to my husband's face. He started laughing again and said he'd been joking and that losing one's tail certainly isn't sex.

"But what is it then?" I asked angrily.

My husband thought about it and said, "Sex is closing your mouth nicely now, not thinking about anything and simply being beautiful."

I was desperate again. Is sex something that you do for others? That seems boring and courteous. Something like a curtsey.

I decided not to turn to my husband any more in this matter. He only makes light of it when I'm being serious.

Yet I sense that I will soon have to take up this subject again. Because lately he seems to be... somehow annoyingly patronising. There isn't the clear, bright closeness of before between us any more. Between us there is now that curtsey, the trap springing... and... clack!... nothing is as it was before.

Stone Chunk
and Beautiful Question

"Who am I?" Stone Chunk asked himself. "Who am I to judge others?" But the judgement had already been made. Stone Chunk had only one more question as gossamer as air, but even that soon vanished. A conviction took shape within him that was as firm as stone – Beautiful Question, my partner for life, really isn't a Beautiful Question, but only a piece of flesh.

Stone Chunk flinched. "And what is that piece of flesh doing now?" he wanted to know.

And the answer that Stone Chunk gave himself was by no means beautiful – "Beautiful Question, who veils herself behind that beautiful name, is giving herself to pleasures of the flesh. For she is after all flesh like me. And what else should flesh do but find ceaseless shameless pleasure in itself?"

Beautiful Question came into the room and didn't know that Stone Chunk had in the meantime come up with an answer. Unsuspectingly she did what came into her head and laughed, for she was cheerful and even a bit frolicsome. She flitted about and sang. Stone Chunk didn't like this at all. He had been taught that where there is flitting about and singing you should look for the basest deceit.

"Beautiful Question," said Stone Chunk, "you're interesting."

Beautiful Question gave a start and swept her straight northland Finno-Ugric hair in a great ark over her head. But her hair didn't fall down again. It remained standing straight up on her head. "Hair, hair, fall down now, won't you?" Beautiful Question pleaded, laughing. But her hair stayed standing up on end as if something had frightened it from the root to the tip of every strand.

Beautiful Question smiled and decided to take what she had just heard as a compliment, although she wasn't really sure. "That's grand," she thought, "that I'm so interesting to him, But I wonder why my hair got such a terrible fright?"

"Yes, interesting that it's so interesting..." Stone Chunk procrastinated and looked at Beautiful Question with his one angry answering eye. Beautiful Question smiled again, but her heart skipped a few beats. "Heart-heart, what's this all about!" Beautiful Question protested. But her heart continued in some strange self-determined rhythm. Beautiful Question kindly offered Stone Chunk a cup of tea.

When Stone Chunk told Beautiful Question for the third time that she was interesting, her blood began to curdle at the sound of his voice. "Blood-blood, why have you started to curdle like this?" she asked herself.

"Stupid Question," grunted Blood. "That Stone Chunk has secretly come up with an answer to you. And a very wrong answer."

"Well, what a very interesting story," thought Beautiful Question. "Hair and Heart and Blood fear that I've been answered wrongly. But this Stone Chunk here said nothing more than that I'm interesting. Interesting, what could he have meant by that?"

Winter came, the sea froze over and boats didn't sail anymore between the rest of the world and the home of Stone Chunk and Beautiful Question. And one evening Stone Chunk told Beautiful Question right to her face, "You're really not Beautiful Question, you're a Piece of Flesh." Beautiful Question's smile was smothered. "That is the answer then that Hair and Heart and Blood warned me about!"

"And you're not Stone Chunk," she screamed angrily, "You're, you're... Wrong Answer!"

And so Beautiful Question, who to Stone Chunk's mind was a Piece of Flesh, and Stone Chunk, who to Beautiful Question's mind was Wrong Answer, lived together for some time.

And Beautiful Question's Hair began to go grey with horror and Blood to flow more and more carefully and Heart often did that rhythm trick. And Beauty began to gradually peel off from Question, for Answer's Wrong flayed her and scraped her – rawly and lusting for flesh.

But a Question remained. That Question was, "Why, on that beautiful evening, was I answered so wrongly?" And Beautiful Question continued to repeat that not at all beautiful question to herself for a long time, hoping that somewhere within her an answer would be born.

But the answer wasn't born. Not yet. Instead Stone Chunk swaggered day after day with his wrong answer. And as soon as Beautiful Question was herself again – beautiful all over and question all over, Stone Chunk came out with his wrong answer. He boasted again and again, "I love truth and I love daring. And even if the truth isn't beautiful, I dare to say it out loud. You are Piece of Flesh, who veils herself behind that beautiful question. I dare say I know, for I'm Stone Chunk and I know how to be objective even if there's no profit in it for me." So swaggered Stone Chunk. And he also said, "My whole life is dedicated to the truth."

For Beautiful Question this truth was nothing other than a base and cruel accusation. She ran out of the room. It was an oh so moonlit night! Water sparkled serenely in the sea and it was so quiet that Beautiful Question's every breath could be heard a long way off. Beautiful Question tried to dance a little, for to her mind this silence was the most beautiful music. And she did dance and before long found herself in an altogether different kind of time and space. And very soon an Answer began to ripen within her. An Answer that was only one of many, but certainly not wrong.

So It's Finally Happened

So it's finally happened. Today I smiled falsely for the first time. It seemed easier that way. At that very moment a gust of wind smashed the gable window of my farmhouse to bits. Gathering up the shards of glass I felt sad about that good old windowpane from the time of the first Estonian republic. It can never be made whole again. And about the fact that I had managed to refrain from smiling falsely for twenty years, but now I'd done it anyway.

An hour later I did it again and in the evening I did it a third time. Cracks appeared in truly being myself, and every new false smile was an irreparable crack in the gable window of my integrity. A few more grimaced smiles and there's going to be a shattering, and the autumn winds will blow in.

Diary of Fear

11 March 2018

This morning I started to be afraid of you too. You had a painful and desperate air. All your nerve endings were suddenly visible. All your anxiety mixed with fear had suddenly melted out from under the snow.

12 March 2018

I'm trying to force myself to be calm. I'm striving to instil the idea in myself that this is life as it is and sooner or later the side that is difficult for others and even oneself to bear becomes visible in everyone. But it doesn't help, doesn't help, doesn't help. My fear of you keeps growing.

13 March 2018

Today I packed my bags. I tried to leave before you came home. I stood at the door and looked back at our life together. At the beginning I'd been so happy. As always.

Suddenly the gate creaked. Your heavy steps came closer along the frozen gravel. We stood facing each other. I looked at you for the last time. I was startled to feel that my fear had gone. You were just as flourishing, dashing and bright as when we first met. I unpacked my bags. We started to live together again.

30 November 2018

But now you've started to be afraid of me. And you can't and you can't get over it. You're afraid that I might pack my bags again when you're away and try to make a run for it.

12 December 2018

Today you did it yourself. You packed up your half of our life and slipped away on the last train over the blackening ridge.

I arrived home at nightfall. The last leaves fell from the poplars we had planted together. A desolate wind was blowing everywhere. For me it was cold even in the warmth of our room. Fear had yet again vanquished love.

Wedded to Myself

1

By morning my husband's black beard had gone bluish-grey. I had tormented him all night long. I don't really know what to say other than – pity. I'd only told him that I was inviting him to a wedding – a wedding where I was getting married to myself. I showed him my wedding dress as well. It was sun-yellow and, using dye on the skirt, I had drawn the most beautiful moments of my life.

"Please, please, put it away!" my husband said. "It's blinding me! There's a strange feeling coming over me and...a sick feeling."

"No, look at it, take a good, close look!" I demanded.

"Put it away, I beg you!" he whined.

"But why?" I slipped into the dress and stood before him.

He cried out. Covered his eyes with his hands and... seemed to break. I went on standing there in all my beauty, my many-coloured gaiety and complexity.

Every time my husband opened his eyes, he was struck by a fresh attack. It was as if he wanted to ask something, but wasn't able to and just moved his mouth.

"Go on, ask, ask away," I encouraged, and continued standing there.

2

My wedding was the most joyous get together any of my friends and acquaintances had ever been to. And all that joy suddenly came together in me. I had never felt that smiling could be so easy.

Only my husband was gloomy. He sat by himself in the corner and every time he looked at me he groaned out loud. I went over to him and stroked his hair and bluish beard.

"Why did you..." His voice broke off. "Why, after all our beautiful years together, did you suddenly need to marry yourself?"

"Why, why! Who needs to ask such questions?" I reproached him and danced off.

"I don't... I don't want to live with you any more if you're going to be like that," he called after me.

I thought then that he was only having me on. Why should my husband be disturbed by my marriage to myself? But he was deadly serious. He saw things in a totally different way. We got a divorce.

3

Five years later we met again. It turned out that my former husband had a candidate of sciences degree in the study of cannibalism. His beard had in the mean time turned quite blue. We sat there – he sombre blue, I still golden yellow.

"Have you married again?" I asked.

"Oh yes, several times. And you? Still married to yourself?"

"Yes, still," I said, uneasily for some reason.

Suddenly I understood that I still felt an inexplicably strong attraction to my former husband.

"I have to carry out some... practical work. Would you help me with it?" he asked.

"Ahh – no!" I heard myself answer. My voice sounded tantalising.

"At least come to my exhibition!" he called out insistently. "The opening is in the tower room of the Academy of Sciences tonight at one o' clock."

"Ehhh... very well," I heard myself answer again.

4

I already knew what would be in the exhibtion. Dresses. The wedding dresses of his former wives. All of them as beautiful and colourfully gay as my own. In a strange way I was attracted, oh, how I was attracted to that exhibition.

"Put on your yellow wedding dress!" he had said. "It doesn't blind me any more."

As if in a trance I climbed up the spiral staircase towards the tower room. What on earth am I doing?

At the very last moment I decided I'd rather jump out of the window than step into that exhibition room and straight in between the sharpened teeth of my former husband.

I stood on the broad windowsill beside the room. I pushed the window open and jumped into the dark autumn night. The flight was long. I was beginning to think it would never end. Suddenly I found myself amid a soft, rustling pile of leaves. A gardener was bending over me. We kissed and drove away from there. If we haven't died, we'll be living quite tolerably ever after.

My former husband defended his doctoral dissertation quite nicely without me, and by all accounts is working on his twelfth marriage. We women feel so easily that we need to feed our men with ourselves and leave all the gaily coloured dresses, which we had taken such great pains to acquire, to adorn their collections.

I'm still married to myself, but now I have a gardener and lover who isn't troubled in the slightest by my unquenchable devotion to myself.

Evening Rendezvous

"In and of itself I am quite religious," said Happiness Formula, grabbed hold of a pine branch with two fingers, broke it off, stuck it between his lips and looked down at Life Story with a smug look.

Life Story lay on her side in front of him in the soft grass and when Happiness Formula leaned his back against the trunk of the pine tree and stretched a little she saw a bright lilac strip of sky above the sea beyond, a bluish pier and the burning-red noddles of a couple of sea-buoys.

"I'm quite religious," he repeated, "but that doesn't mean that my behaviour is always seemly. I must admit that I'm actually a great ninny."

Life Story gave a start. "I'd like to know why you invited me here today."

Happiness Fomula laughed. He looked at Life Story and said slowly, "I suppose to have a bit of fun with you." He grabbed hold of Life Story's slender ankle, lifted the sole of her foot to his mouth and tickled it with the pine branch.

Life Story pulled her foot away. "Aren't you straightforward. But so be it. Doesn't particularly interest me." Life Story turned her back to him and continued to admire the lilac strip of sky, the pier and the fire-red sea buoys. Something rustled at the top of the tree. A strange chattering and grinding could be heard.

Happiness Formula fell silent and looked covetously at Life Story's graceful back.

"You entice everyone. Everyone," said Life Story. "Life Stories bend according to you, turn and twist. You spoil them a little and then leave them behind. And we end our Stories – disappointed, confused, unhappy and without a single formula. Without a single blasted formula!" She felt Happiness Formula's hot breath on the nape of her neck. It intoxicated her. Happiness Formula put his hand on Life Story's neck. "A mosquito's bitten you!" He poked Life Story's cheek with the pine branch. "And it's still biting you..." he whispered.

Life Story turned round and looked angrily into Happiness Formula's wantonly flashing eyes. "I'm not a woman. And you're not a man. And even if we were, you know very well how dangerous it is to expect happiness from someone else. You can't even expect happiness from yourself. A Life Story has to concentrate on something else, certainly not on happiness and certainly not on a formula. Then maybe... But don't come enticing me with scented envelopes, thermal socks, favourite ice cream and your There's-A-Remedy-For-Every-Pain philosophy."

"There's a lot more to me than favourite ice cream and thermal socks," Happiness Formula said.

"Right. But I'm happier without you."

And Life Story went away. And down from the pine tree onto her shoulder jumped her Brain's Monkey. And from somewhere high up her Love's Red Pheasant landed on her other shoulder. And she went to look after the garden where her Monkey and Pheasant liked to live. And one evening, when her Monkey was already sleeping, Happiness Formula came like a spring rain. They met unexpectedly on the bluish pier and by the lustre of the Red Pheasant's feathers and the red sea-buoys Life Story peeled the Formula off Happiness and Happiness carefully released Life from her Story. They remained as Happiness and Life, who became part of one another on that darkening pier. Not a single word, or mosquito, or pine branch.

About the Author

Kristiina Ehin is one of Estonia's leading poets and is known throughout Europe for her poetry and short stories. She has an MA in Comparative and Estonian Folklore from the University of Tartu, and folklore plays a significant role in her work. In her native Estonian she has to date published six volumes of poetry, three books of short stories and a retelling of South-Estonian fairy tales. She has also written two theatrical productions as well as poetic, imaginative radio broadcasts, one of which has also been released as a CD. She has won Estonia's most prestigious poetry prize for *Kaitseala* (Huma, 2005), a book of poems and journal entries written during a year spent as a nature reserve warden on an otherwise uninhabited island off Estonia's north coast.

Walker on Water is Kristiina's eleventh book in English translation. She has previously published seven books of poetry and three of prose. The *Drums of Silence* (Oleander, 2007) was awarded the British Poetry Society Popescu Prize for European Poetry in Translation, and *The Scent of Your Shadow* (Arc, 2010) is a British Poetry Book Society Recommended Translation. *1001 Winters* (Bitter Oleander Press, 2013) was nominated for the Poetry Society Popescu Prize.

Her plays and broadcasts have also been translated into English and her work, poetry and prose, appears regularly in leading English language literary magazines and anthologies in the US, UK and Ireland. In addition to English, her work has been translated into 20 languages. She is a highly acclaimed performer of her poetry, prose and drama and travels extensively around Estonia and abroad to perform her work, sometimes accompanied by musicians.

Kristiina lives with her husband, the musician Silver Sepp, and her son in Tartu, Estonia.

About the Translator

Ilmar Lehtpere is Kristiina Ehin's English language translator. He has translated nearly all of her work – poetry, prose and drama – most of which has appeared in Kristiina's eleven books in his translation, as well as in numerous English language literary magazines. Kristiina and he have won two prestigious prizes together for poetry in translation and have been nominated for another. Their collaboration is ongoing. His own poetry has appeared in Estonian and Irish literary magazines, and *Wandering Towards Dawn* (Lapwing) is a volume of his and Sadie Murphy's poetry.

Also Available from The Unnamed Press

The Unnamed Press publishes literature, comics and lost classics from around the world.

Nigerians in Space
Deji Olukotun

"Fast-paced, well-written and packed with insight and humor. Olukotun is a very talented storyteller."
—Charles Yu

International Crime Fiction, Paperback, $16.99, 978-1-939419-01-9

Good Night, Mr. Kissinger
K. Anis Ahmed

"Vividly realized and intricately observed, Good Night, Mr. Kissinger *is a poignant portrait of a city and the characters that live in the wake of great change."*
—Tahmima Anam, author of *The Good Muslim*

Fiction, Paperback, $16.00, 978-1-939419-04-0

CPSIA information can be obtained at www.ICGtesting.com
Printed in the USA
BVOW04s1458280914

368542BV00002B/3/P